GHOSTLY TERRORS

Daniel Cohen

Illustrated with photographs and drawings

A MINSTREL® BOOK

PUBLISHED BY POCKET BOOKS

New York   London   Toronto   Sydney   Tokyo   Singapore

PICTURE CREDITS

Aldus Archives, 109; Dover Publications, Inc., 8, 27, 35, 95, 105, 115; Robert Estall, 103; *Illustrated Police News,* 1872, 71; New York Public Library Picture Collection, 17, 33, 39, 51, 56–57, 65, 75, 76, 79, 81, 87, 90, 122. Drawings on pages 13, 53, and 119 by Ondré Pettingili.

A Minstrel Book published by
POCKET BOOKS, a division of Simon & Schuster
1230 Avenue of the Americas, New York, NY 10020

ISBN: 0-671-70507-5

First Minstrel Books printing June 1990

10 9 8 7 6 5 4

A MINSTREL BOOK and colophon are registered trademarks of Simon & Schuster

Printed in the U.S.A.

CONTENTS

Introduction

TERRORS IN
THE NIGHT

All the best ghost stories are true. At least they are *supposed* to be true. For centuries people have sat around at night and told one another ghost stories. Usually the storyteller will insist that the tale he is about to relate really happened. It makes the story more exciting to believe that it happened.

All of the stories in this book are supposed to have really happened. And maybe they did. But there is no proof that they happened as told. On the other hand, there is no proof that they didn't. Some people believe them. Others take them as just stories. You may believe them or not as you wish.

Do I believe them? Well, yes and no. In the middle of a nice sunny afternoon I am very brave, very much in control. I don't jump at strange noises or worry about moving shadows. At such times I say I don't believe in ghosts. All these ghost tales are merely legends. They are repeated not because they are true, but because they are good stories.

That's how I feel in the middle of a nice sunny afternoon. At night, with a storm howling outside, I can feel very differently. Then all of these stories seem a lot more possible. I wonder if that thumping sound is just a branch blowing against a window or ghostly footsteps coming up the stairs.

At one time it was traditional to tell ghost stories on Christmas Eve. Today ghost stories are repeated at slumber parties or around campfires. And they are often read at night before going to bed—but perhaps not to sleep.

For your entertainment I present an unlucky thirteen tales of ghostly ghosts, walking corpses, screaming skulls, and other supernatural horrors. One dark night you may be able to scare your friends with these tales. But you will have to scare yourself first by reading them.

1

THE PASSENGER
IN BLACK

This little tale was one of the favorites of Lord Halifax. He was a celebrated English collector of ghostly tales. Each Christmas he would bring down his collection and read from it. The stories would terrify, and delight, his own children, and any others who happened to be staying with them.

The story concerns a certain Colonel Ewart, the relative of a close friend of Lord Halifax. The Colonel was a rather stuffy man. He didn't like traveling on trains. What he disliked most was sharing his compartment with strangers. But sometimes a trip was necessary.

One day the Colonel had to take a train from the city of Carlisle to London. When he arrived at the train station he was relieved to find that the train was not crowded. He found an empty compartment without much trouble.

Alone, the Colonel was happy. He took off his coat and boots in order to be more comfortable. Then he took out a copy of the *Times*, and settled down for a pleasant journey.

The trip was a long one. The train was warm, and it rocked gently as it sped toward London. The Colonel found himself dozing over his newspaper. Soon the paper slipped from his hands and he was fast asleep.

Colonel Ewart awoke slowly. He was not sure how long he had been asleep. It must have been for over an hour. He had slept very soundly. But now his neck and back were stiff and his mouth was very dry. The Colonel looked for his newspaper. It was then that he first realized he was no longer alone in his compartment.

Sitting across from him was a woman in a black dress. Her face was almost completely hidden by a thick black veil. The Colonel had no idea how this woman could have gotten into the compartment without waking him. That, however, was not his first concern.

Colonel Ewart was a very proper gentleman. It was not proper for a gentleman to sit in the same compartment with a lady without his coat and boots. He quickly pulled on his coat and fumbled for his boots.

"I'm sorry," he mumbled. "I didn't realize you had come in. I thought I was alone."

The woman in black said nothing.

Thinking his fellow passenger might be a bit deaf, the Colonel repeated his apology more loudly this time. Still she did not reply. The woman in black did not even look up at him. She seemed to be staring at her lap, at something hidden in the folds of her skirt.

Then the woman began rocking back and forth. And she started to sing softly as well. Colonel Ewart could not make out the words of the song, but they sounded familiar, like some sort of lullaby. He was suddenly struck by the fear that she had a baby with her.

Sitting across from him was a woman in a black dress.

The Colonel hated babies. He imagined an infant crying and screaming all the way to London.

Whatever the woman was holding, she was holding it very closely. He was unable to see what she had in her lap. If she was traveling with a baby, surely she must have some equipment for it. He reflected that most new mothers seemed to need trunkloads of equipment for even the shortest trip. He could see no sign of this. Indeed he could see no luggage of any kind in the compartment except his own. Stranger and stranger, Colonel Ewart thought.

He was not ordinarily a curious man. But this woman had aroused what curiosity he had. He really did want to see what she held in her lap.

Suddenly all curious thoughts were wiped from his mind. There was a screech of metal wheels against metal rails. This was followed by a crash and a terrific jolt. Colonel Ewart was thrown violently backward and then forward. His suitcase was knocked from the rack, and struck him sharply on the head. For a moment the Colonel was unconscious.

When he awoke he realized there had been a train accident. As a military man, the Colonel had faced physical danger many times. He did not panic. He rose slowly. His only injury seemed to be a bump on the head where he had been hit by the suitcase. Then he carefully left the compartment.

Outside everything was in confusion. People were running about shouting. At the front end of the train there had been some injuries. The Colonel went forward to see if he could help. Then he remembered the woman in the black dress. He rushed back to the compartment in which he had been sitting. It was empty. He realized that he did not see her after the crash. Perhaps she had fled before he awoke.

The Colonel searched among the passengers who were wandering about outside the train. He could not find her. He talked to the trainmen. They had not seen her either. No one had seen her.

Moreover, the trainmen told the Colonel that after he had boarded the train at Carlisle his compartment door had been locked. That was customary. No one could have entered his compartment. Yet he had clearly seen the woman in black. He was puzzled and deeply troubled. The trainmen acted oddly. They did not want to talk about what might have happened.

It was several months before Colonel Ewart learned the awful truth. He had described his experience many times. One day he told it to a railway official that he met. Upon hearing the story, the man turned pale.

"So it happened again," the official said.

"What happened again?" demanded the Colonel.

The railway official said that a few years before Colonel Ewart's meeting with the passenger in black, there had been a particularly horrible accident on the Carlisle to London run.

A bride and bridegroom had been traveling on the line. It was the young man's first trip

Colonel Ewart did not like traveling on trains.

to London. He wanted to see everything. He
stuck his head too far out of the window, and
it was caught by a wire. The impact completely severed his head. The headless body
fell back into his young bride's lap.

No one else on the train knew what had
happened until the train pulled in to London.
They found the young woman sitting in the
compartment holding her husband's headless

17

body. She was rocking back and forth, and singing a lullaby to it. The shock had driven her completely mad.

The poor lady was committed to an institution, but she lived only a few months. She never regained her sanity. She would sit for hours on end, rocking back and forth, singing the same lullaby.

From time to time after her death passengers on the Carlisle to London train had reported seeing the tragic, and awful, figure.

2

BURIED ALIVE

Imagine this. You are in an accident and you are knocked unconscious. But you look as if you are dead. Everybody thinks you are dead. So, with a lot of weeping and wailing, they bury you. Then you wake up in a coffin, six feet underground. What would you do? What *could* you do?

That thought is one of the most horrible that anyone can imagine.

Don't worry about it now. It won't happen to you. Today doctors can be absolutely sure you are dead before you are buried. Machines can even keep people who are really dead breathing. Besides, if you weren't really dead before the undertaker embalmed you, you certainly would be dead when he was finished.

It wasn't always this way. At one time corpses were not embalmed. They were just buried, and quickly too. Doctors could not always be absolutely sure if a patient was dead or just unconscious. Often there were no doctors around. There are a number of cases of persons who were thought to be "dead" coming back to life. So being buried alive was a small, but real, possibility.

In the nineteenth century there were a number of coffins designed with built-in signaling devices. If you woke up in the coffin you could pull a rope that would ring a bell above ground. I have never heard of a case in which such a device was used successfully. But there were plenty of stories about being buried alive. Here are a few of them.

There is the tale of the young woman who became very ill with typhoid fever. People

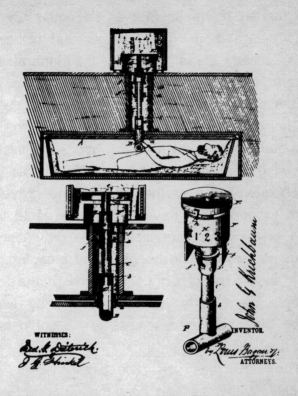

A patented device to prevent people from being buried alive.

were sure that she was going to die. They tried to contact members of her family.

Her oldest brother was a long way off when he heard of his sister's grave illness.

He rushed home as fast as he could. By the time he got home he was told that his sister was already dead. In fact, the funeral had taken place that very afternoon, and he had just missed it.

The grief-stricken brother hurried to the cemetery. The gravediggers had just finished throwing the last shovelful of earth into the fresh grave. The brother begged the gravediggers to open the grave so that he could take one last look at his sister. The gravediggers refused. He kept on begging and pleading. He was such a pitiful sight that some of the local people came over and said that they would open the grave themselves, so he could have his final look.

The earth was soft. The digging went very quickly. Within half an hour the coffin was uncovered and opened. The mourning brother looked down at his sister for what he thought would be the last time. Then one of the people who had been standing around said that he saw the "corpse" move. Others saw it move. People began whispering excitedly to one another. The "corpse" moved more violently. Then the "corpse" actually sat up, and finally stepped out of her coffin. The young woman had not been dead at all. People fearing the spread of deadly typhoid fever had buried her too quickly.

The young woman recovered and, according to the story, she lived on for many years after her "death" and raised a large family.

A more ghostly tale is told about a man named Samuel Jocelyn of North Carolina. He wasn't quite as lucky as the young woman either. Jocelyn was thrown from his horse, struck his head on a rock, and was pronounced dead by a local doctor. Since he was supposed to be dead, Jocelyn was appropriately, and quickly, buried.

A couple of nights after the funeral Jocelyn's old friend, Alexander Hostler, was troubled with a bad dream. He dreamed that his friend Jocelyn appeared before him.

"How could you let me be buried when I was not dead?" said the shade of Jocelyn.

"But you *were* dead," answered Hostler.

"No, I wasn't," replied the ghost. "Open my coffin. You will see that I am not lying the way that I was buried."

Hostler tried to ignore the dream. But he had the same dream again the next night, and the next. It was driving him crazy. He was afraid to go to sleep. Finally, he couldn't stand it anymore. He persuaded a friend to go with him to the graveyard at night. The two dug up Jocelyn's grave. They opened the coffin lid. Jocelyn had been buried, just like everyone else, face up. But now the corpse was lying face down. Somehow the body had turned over.

An even more ghostly story of being buried alive goes this way:

One evening a storekeeper in a small southern town had a very strange customer. She was a thin pale young woman dressed all in gray. She didn't speak, but just pointed at a bottle of milk. The storekeeper gave her the milk. She took it and walked away quickly without paying or even saying thank you. There was something about the way she looked that made the storekeeper feel very uncomfortable, even frightened. He was afraid to ask her for money.

The following evening the same young woman walked into the store. Again she pointed at a bottle of milk. Again the storekeeper gave it to her without asking her to pay.

By this time the storekeeper knew that something very strange, perhaps very terrible, was happening. The next evening he made sure that he had a couple of his friends in the store as witnesses. The woman in gray appeared as she had on the two previous nights. As before, she pointed to a bottle of milk. As before, the storekeeper gave it to her, but this time when she left, the storekeeper and his friends followed her.

She walked very quickly down the main street, with the men following close behind. The woman in gray never looked back. She did not even seem to notice them. She turned down a side street, then another. Even before she reached her destination, the men knew where she was headed. The woman in gray was quickly leading them to the graveyard.

She entered the graveyard. The men following her were all badly frightened now, but somehow they could not stop. The woman in gray paused in front of a particular grave. Then she just disappeared.

The grave that she had stopped in front of was a newly dug one. The men got shovels and began to dig. When they uncovered the coffin and opened it, they found that it contained two corpses—that of a young mother and her infant. Both had died of fever a few days before. They were poor strangers, and so had been buried in a common grave without any ceremony.

The corpse of the young mother was clothed in a gray dress, and was the image of the woman who had come to the store. But she was undoubtedly dead. As the men stared in shock and disbelief into the open

In Memory of
Mary the Wife of
Simeon Harvey
Who Departed this
Life Decembr 20th
1785 In 39th year of
Her age on her left
Arm lieth the Infant
Which was still

Headstone for burial of a mother and child.

coffin, they saw something move. It was the child, weak and ill but still alive.

As they reached in to take the child from the coffin, the men saw that the coffin also contained three empty milk bottles.

3

THE MISSING CORPSE

Fear of being buried alive also plays a part in this odd and eerie little tale. It is said to have taken place during the early years of this century.

It's about an ex-army man named Winterton. After years of drinking and fast living, Winterton wound up living in a little room in a cheap part of Damascus, Syria. He made a small living as a tourist guide.

Winterton's best friend was an Arab shopkeeper named Hassan. The two men shared a serious interest in psychic phenomena and life after death. They had both heard stories in which the spirit of a person at the point of death, or recently dead, had appeared to a friend many miles away. The two men made a pact. Whoever died first was to try and contact the other.

It looked as if Winterton was to be the first. A severe cholera epidemic swept through Damascus. Winterton fell victim to the disease. He was taken to the hospital, but there was little hope for him. Most victims of the disease died quickly.

Hassan did not try to visit his friend. No visitors were allowed in the hospital during an epidemic. Besides, there was always the possibility of catching the disease himself. In a few days Hassan heard that Winterton had died.

Hassan was saddened by news of his friend's death. He thought of the pact they had made. For that reason he was not too surprised to see Winterton appear in his room at about seven that very night. Winterton looked much the same as he always had.

"I'm so sorry that you are dead, my friend,"

said Hassan. "When I heard the terrible news I could hardly believe it."

"I'm not dead," said the form of Winterton calmly. "That's why I have come to you. They only think I am dead. I'm sure I will recover. But they are going to bury me. You must stop them."

Hassan knew what the conditions in the hospital were during an epidemic. The few doctors and nurses were badly overworked. They did not have time to treat each patient carefully. Most died, no matter what they did. Under such conditions it was quite possible for a still living but unconscious person to be thought dead. Mistakes happen.

The form of Winterton described how he had been pronounced dead. Then he had been loaded onto a cart and taken to the mortuary. "Can you imagine what it is like to lie among all those bodies?" he said. "I must get out of that place. If I don't, they will bury me alive."

As Winterton talked, his form began to fade. Soon it had disappeared entirely. Hassan did not know what to think. The experience had shaken him badly.

He began to worry. Perhaps the form of Winterton had been telling the truth. Perhaps he really wasn't dead. Hassan knew he had to do something—but what?

Early the next morning Hassan went to the hospital. The doctor could not remember Winterton. All he knew was that several people had died the previous day and had been taken to the mortuary. There they were to remain overnight. It was dangerous to keep the corpses of cholera victims around for long. They would be buried that very day.

Hassan rushed to the mortuary. The mortuary keeper, an old man, was alone. Hassan described his friend and the old man said he remembered such a body. Hassan knew there was a risk of infection in entering the mortuary. But he had to see his friend's body. He had to know if Winterton was really dead, and the "ghost" he saw was just an hallucination.

The old mortuary keeper did not want to let

During epidemics the dead are taken away quickly.

him in. Even a bribe was refused. The old man told Hassan that walking among all those cholera victims was dangerous. Hassan agreed that it was, but he was willing to take the risk. The mortuary keeper raised more objections. Hassan brushed them aside.

"It is not against the law," he said. "All I

want to do is see the body. It has not been taken for burial yet, has it?"

The mortuary keeper looked even more uncomfortable. Finally, he said, "To tell the truth, I am not sure."

"What do you mean, you are not sure? It's your job to know these things."

"That body has disappeared. I saw it brought in yesterday and put on a table. Then I stepped out for a little drink. I know it is against the rules, but this is a hard job. I locked the door, of course. When I came back that body was gone. There was nothing of value on the body. Who would steal it?"

"About what time did this happen?" asked Hassan.

"I went out at about seven."

Hassan recalled that was the time that Winterton's form had appeared to him.

Hassan was angry now. "Do you mean to tell me a corpse just got up and walked out?" he shouted.

"Oh, no," said the mortuary keeper. "I told you the door was locked. But there is the

In the Middle Ages, people tried to ward off epidemic diseases by dancing in the graveyard.

ventilator. When I left it was closed. When I came back it was open.''

Hassan looked at the ventilator. Winterton had always been a very thin man. It was possible, just possible, that he could have squeezed through the narrow opening.

''Please don't tell anyone,'' pleaded the old

man. "If it is learned that I left the mortuary unattended I'll lose my job. Where will I ever find another at my age?"

Hassan was deep in his own thoughts. If he had come when the form of Winterton had appeared to him he might have been able to save his old friend. Now there was no way of telling what would happen. If Winterton had escaped from the mortuary he would still be in the advanced stages of cholera. Wandering the streets alone, he could not survive for long. He was probably dead already.

Hassan assured the old man that he would tell no one. "It is not your fault," he said. "If anyone is to blame, it is me. I should have come sooner."

Sadly, Hassan went back to his shop. Winterton's corpse was never found. Nor did his spirit again appear to Hassan. No one knows exactly what happened.

4

THREE IN A BED

There are many versions of this particular story. It is no longer possible to tell which is the original. This is the way I first heard it.

It was shortly after World War II. John Pomroy had been discharged from the army. His third day out of uniform he married Anne Norton. John and Anne had known one another for years. They had been engaged since he had come home on leave for a few days during the dark winter of 1943.

Before the war John had been a moderately successful commercial artist in New

York City. Magazines and advertising agencies provided him with a steady stream of work.

John, however, was never happy with this life. He had always wanted to be a painter. Now, with several years of painful war experiences behind him, he felt that he could not face the commercial art world again. He had saved some money. What he wanted to do was to buy a place in the country and just paint for a while.

This decision pleased Anne. She, too, was a painter who had tired of city life. The grim war years had also given her the desire to get out into the country where nature was still beautiful. They had often written to one another about this shared dream. Now they were going to do it.

Finding the right house was less of a problem than they had expected. They only had to look for two days. The real estate agent showed them a large country house about 90 miles to the north and west of New York City. It was airy and well lighted, with plenty of room for a large studio. The house had

The couple moved into a large, old house.

more room than they really needed. But the
setting was so pleasant, and the price so rea-
sonable, that John and Anne decided to take
it anyway. The top part of the house could
always be closed up.

John and Anne were very happy with their
house. They would have been completely
happy with it were it not for one little thing.
They often took a walk in the evening. When
they returned they sometimes saw a light in
the unused upper part of the house.

John investigated, but found nothing. He removed the fuses for the upper part of the house, and took out all the light bulbs. But still, if they looked up at the top of the house some evenings, there was the light. It was eerie. Finally, John decided it was some sort of optical illusion. Anne was not so sure.

No one who has a large house in the country will be left alone for long—especially when the weather turns nice.

An old army buddy of John's was the first visitor. The ground floor was completely taken up with living quarters and studio. In order to accommodate their guest, John and Anne put him in a room on the second floor. John had replaced the fuses and the light bulbs. Anne had cleaned and aired the room, and put fresh sheets on the bed. Though it had been unused for months, perhaps years, it seemed very pleasant.

John had almost forgotten about the strange lights. Anne remembered, but said nothing.

The visitor had gotten lost on the way to

the house. He arrived when it was quite late, and everyone was tired. John and Anne insisted that he go directly to bed. They could talk in the morning.

The next morning at breakfast the visitor looked even worse than he had the night before. He looked as though he hadn't slept at all. When he was asked what had happened, he insisted that everything was just fine. Yet it was obvious that something was very wrong.

Then he told John and Anne that he would have to leave at once. They were surprised and hurt, and asked him why. He simply repeated that he would have to leave. Nothing would change his mind and he wouldn't discuss it. Within an hour he was gone. John and Anne were completely puzzled by what had happened.

They did not brood on this puzzle for long. A short time later more visitors arrived. They were a young couple almost the same ages as John and Anne. The four of them had been friends before the war. They had not

Cartoon by the nineteenth-century artist, Cruik-shank. It shows a man who thinks he has seen a ghost. But it is just his clothes hung near his bed.

seen one another for years, and their reunion was a joyous one.

The couple was put in the same upstairs bedroom as the previous visitor. The two went to bed late that night. Since they were both tired, they fell asleep almost immediately.

After about an hour the man woke up. He had a strange and unsettling feeling. He felt his wife asleep on one side. But he also had the impression that there was somebody, or something else, on the other side of him in the bed. This brought on a wave of such unreasoning terror that he was afraid to reach out his hand and touch whatever it was. He was even afraid to turn on the light and look at it.

Instead, he quietly woke his wife. He told her to get out of the bed, and walk to the far side of the room. He followed her. The room was dimly lit by moonlight coming through the open window. They looked back toward the bed. The sheets and blankets were heaped up as if they were covering a human form.

The couple stared at the form but could not make out any details. Then they heard footsteps coming slowly down the hallway outside the room. The footsteps reached the door and stopped. The door handle began to turn slowly and the door started to swing open.

The couple did not know what they would see. They did not want to see anything, so they hid their eyes. They heard the footsteps enter the room. There was silence for a moment. Then came a hideous choking sound from near the bed. The man lowered his hands just in time to see the sheets and blankets twitch and shudder, then slide from the bed onto the floor. The footsteps then retreated back across the room, down the hall, and died away.

There was to be no more sleep that night. The two swore that they would never spend another night in that room. They told John and Anne so the next morning, when they described what they had seen and heard.

John then called the previous visitor. He admitted that he had an identical experience when he stayed in the room. He was simply afraid to talk about it at the time. He didn't want people to think he was crazy.

No one had any explanation for what happened. John and Anne didn't wait around for one either. They sold the house as quickly as they could and moved back to the city.

5

THE HOODED FIGURE

Do evil or tragic events leave some sort of mark on the place where they happened? According to many ghost stories, they do exactly that. A stranger enters a house about which he knows nothing. He is almost overcome by the feeling of evil or violence, yet can find no reason for this feeling. Only later does he learn that some terrible event has taken place in that house.

A good example of this type of tale is the one that psychical researcher and writer Joseph Braddock heard from a friend. The story started in 1941. Britain was at war. Members of the armed forces were being lodged in private homes all over the country.

A group of young officers had been put up in a house in the county of Kent. During the conversation one evening, one of the officers mentioned that he had recently been housed at a fine mansion in the county of Dorset. He was asked to describe the house, which he did.

"Ah," said his host. "I know that house. It is really a beautiful place. You must have enjoyed yourself there."

The young officer looked nervous. Finally, he was forced to admit that he had not enjoyed his stay in Dorset at all.

"Oh, why?"

The young officer became even more embarrassed. Grudgingly, he said that he thought the house had been haunted.

To the officer's surprise his host did not laugh, but said very earnestly, "Please tell me what happened."

"It wasn't anything you could put your finger on," said the young man. "But everyone was oppressed by this feeling of evil. It was so thick you could almost touch it."

Everything had been fine when the army men first came into the house. The owner had moved out. Before he did he had put most of his art treasures in storage. There was only one picture still in the dining room. It was a picture of an older woman wearing the clothes of an earlier time. Regarding the picture, the owner left some very strange instructions. The picture had to stay exactly where it was. It was not to be moved for any reason.

The officers hung a dart board in the dining room. During one game a badly thrown dart nicked the picture frame. The Colonel who was in charge was very angry. He said somebody was going to throw a dart into a valuable picture. So he went against the owner's instructions. He had the painting taken down and stored in the attic. That's when the trouble started.

The men began to feel an evil presence nearby. It was almost as if they were being followed. They never saw anything. But at night they sometimes thought they could see the door handles of their bedrooms moving. The doors never opened. No one ever came in. They were all brave men, but this frightened them.

When they were given orders to move from the house, every officer was heartily glad to get out. No one ever wanted to see the place again, though no one could explain exactly why.

"That's about all there is to it," said the young officer. "It really isn't much of a story."

His host had been looking very serious. He seemed to be considering what course of action to take. Finally he said, "I think that I can throw a little light on what happened. By an odd coincidence, during World War I in 1917, I was sent to Dorset. I was recovering from a wound, and I stayed with an elderly lady in the neighborhood of the house of which you spoke. She told me that the mansion had once been the scene of an awful tragedy."

This story also involved army officers. About 1807 there was a regiment of soldiers quartered in the area. The owner of the mansion asked the General of the regiment to dine at his house. The General was asked to bring one of his young officers with him. There was to be a party with dancing afterwards, and there were several single young ladies who needed partners.

The General, of course, accepted the invitation at once. He took with him a young officer whose family he knew well. The young man had always been one of the brightest and most well-mannered officers in the regiment.

During dinner the young officer was seated at the table between two of the single young ladies. They were both very attractive. And they both tried to make conversation with him. But he completely, even rudely, ignored them. This was quite unlike the young man. Worse still, he was staring directly at his hostess with a look of horror on his face.

The General had no idea what the cause

Uniforms of British soldiers around 1807

of this strange behavior might be. He tried to attract the young man's attention. But it was no use. The General was getting angrier and angrier.

Then, quite suddenly, the officer jumped from his chair, almost knocking it over. He shouted, "I can't stand it any longer," and he rushed from the room.

The General now assumed that the fellow had suddenly gone mad. He followed the young man, not knowing what he would do next. Following was not an easy task. The officer had mounted his horse and was galloping away as if the Devil were pursuing him. But the General had a faster horse. He finally overtook the young man, and grabbed the bridle of his horse, bringing it to a halt.

"What the Devil are you doing?" shouted the General.

"The Devil, that's it!" cried the officer. "I saw a hooded figure standing behind our hostess. The figure was telling her over and over again to commit suicide."

The General was now sure that his junior

The young officer saw a hooded figure.

officer had suddenly gone stark mad. He tried to calm him down. "Nonsense, my boy. Nonsense. It's just your imagination."

They didn't talk for long. A horseman was approaching at breakneck speed. It was one of the footmen from the house.

"Where are you going?" shouted the General.

The footman drew up for a moment. "To get a doctor," he panted. "But I know it is already too late."

"What happened?" asked the General, fearing he knew the answer to that question.

"Just after you left," said the footman, "Madame grabbed a knife, and cut her throat in front of everybody."

6

THE HAUNTED SUBMARINE

There are many tales of bad-luck, jinxed, or even haunted ships. One of the best comes from World War I. It is about a haunted submarine or U-boat.

The U-boat was the weapon with which the Germans hoped to win the war. The U-boats had been very successful at sinking British and American ships. The Germans wanted to build as many U-boats as quickly as they could.

In 1916 a group of 24 U-boats was being built in the shipyard at Bruges in occupied Belgium. Construction was normal for 23 of

these boats. For the 24th, nothing went right. This submarine was known only by its number U-65.

Several workers were killed in mysterious accidents. In October, 1916, when U-65 was finally launched, one of the officers either fell or was swept overboard and was drowned. Something went wrong with the first underwa-

German U-boats of World War I

ter test. The submarine was unable to surface for twelve hours. When it finally did come up the crew was badly shaken. Though U-65 was examined carefully after the accident, no one could figure out what had gone wrong. The day after the accident a torpedo exploded. A second lieutenant and five seamen were blown to bits. Most of the later stories of the haunting centered on this dead second lieutenant.

Rumors about U-65 being a bad-luck ship began to spread. Several crewmen reported seeing the ghost of the second lieutenant. One man said, "We saw him come aboard and walk slowly to the bow. He stood there, staring at us, with his arms folded across his chest."

The U-boat commander first tried to play down such stories. He knew that everyone was under a great strain. "I'm sure it's just imagination. The accident was a sad experience for us all. Just try to put it out of your minds." One man who had seen the ghost could not put it out of his mind. He deserted and was never found.

U-65 was repaired and went back into service. All was normal for a few months. Then people began seeing the ghost again. One of the witnesses was the captain himself. The U-boat docked at Bruges, and the captain and crew went ashore. A short time later there was an Allied air attack on the port city. The captain of U-65 was killed in the bombing.

After that, the fears surrounding U-65 grew even worse. The German navy needed the ship, so the high command tried to calm the crew. The high command knew that a ship with a frightened crew would not be very effective. U-65 was carefully checked again. It was thought that the lighting or some sort of poisonous fumes might be causing hallucinations. Nothing was found.

Admiral Schroeder, head of the U-boat command, was convinced that all the talk of ghosts was "superstitious nonsense." He spent a night alone in the U-boat. The next morning he announced to the crew that he had seen and heard nothing. On the contrary, he had slept very well. The men continued to look gloomy. So the admiral called in a minister to carry out an exorcism of the ship.

What Admiral Schroeder thought the U-boat really needed was a tough new commander. He found one in Lieutenant Commander Gustav Schelle. Commander Schelle announced that anyone on his ship who talked of hauntings and ghosts would be severely punished.

For the next year U-65 became an effective weapon of war. Nothing out of the ordinary happened. Then came May, 1918, and the ghost returned. This time the terror was worse than ever.

The first man to feel it was Master Gunner Erich Eberhardt. He was one of Commander Schelle's most trusted officers. One evening Eberhardt rushed into the control room screaming, "I've seen the ghost—an officer standing near the bow torpedo tubes. He brushed past me and disappeared!"

The Master Gunner was so hysterical that he had to be locked up. After a few hours he seemed to quiet down and recover. He was released and as soon as he got free he grabbed a bayonet and stabbed himself to death.

A short time later another of Captain Schelle's close associates, Chief Petty Officer Richard Meyer, was swept overboard. His body was never recovered.

The crew was now thoroughly demoralized.

Admiral Schroeder

Instead of seeking out the enemy as they were supposed to do, they avoided all contact. The U-boat was struck by shellfire anyway, and had to limp back to Bruges for repairs.

Admiral Schroeder was enraged. Even the iron-nerved Commander Schelle seemed to be afraid of ghosts now. He had Schelle and every other officer of U-65 removed. When she set out again, in mid-1918, U-65 had an entirely new staff of officers. But apparently that did not improve things.

The end of U-65 was quite mysterious. On the morning of July 10, 1918, an American submarine patrolling off southern Ireland saw a U-boat lying on its side on the surface. The ship was identified as the U-65.

At first, the Americans thought the ship might be a decoy. They watched it carefully for quite a while. Nothing seemed to move. So the American captain decided to blow the ship up. As they were preparing their torpedos, the U-65 was torn apart by an explosion.

Was the U-65 a decoy filled with explosives that went off too soon? Or was there some other reason for the explosion? Just before she blew up, the American captain thought he saw someone standing on the U-boat near the bow. The man did not move. He just stood there with his arms folded. He appeared to be an officer, and was wearing a navy overcoat.

The war ended four months later. All of the other U-boats surrendered peacefully.

The case of the U-65 has been investigated many times, both by German authorities and others. No one has yet come up with a completely satisfactory explanation for all the strange and terrible things that happened.

7

GHOSTLY WARNINGS

It is said that the ghost of Frederick the Great of Prussia appeared to his nephew, Frederick William. Frederick William was at that time the ruler of the German state of Prussia. He had sent his armies to invade France. Frederick William thought the invasion was very wise. The ghost of his famous uncle knew better.

"Unless you call off the Prussian army from Paris, nephew," said the spirit, "you may expect to see someone who will not be welcome to you."

Poor Frederick William was terrified. He was

self he changed his mind about the White Lady. She was seen several times in 1806. A few days later Prince Louis of Prussia was killed in a battle with Napoleon's army.

There was also a reported sighting of the White Lady in June, 1914. The ruler at that time was Kaiser Wilhelm II. The Kaiser didn't die. But his relative, Archduke Francis Ferdinand, was assassinated late in June. That was the spark for the start of World War I. The Kaiser survived the war. But Germany lost the war and the German monarchy was destroyed forever.

Many other families have stories of ghostly figures that warn of coming death. These ghostly warnings come in many forms. They may be ladies in white or gray. The family of the poet Lord Byron was said to learn of the doom of one of its members when a ghost, called The Black Friar, appeared. This ghost was said to wander the cloisters of Newstead Abbey.

Sometimes these death warnings look much

Ghosts often warn of a coming death. Here a ghost appears to a servant of the Duke of Buckingham. A short time later the Duke died.

more frightening than a white lady or a black monk. The Kinchardines family of Scotland is said to be warned of death by something called the "specter of the bloody hand."

Often the warnings are not in human form

at all. Members of the Vaughn family are supposed to see a black dog before one of them dies. There is a sad story about a member of the family who did not believe in this legend. But then he didn't exactly disbelieve it either. He did not tell his wife about it because he did not want to frighten her.

One of his children was ill with smallpox. It seemed to be a mild case. Still, the disease is dangerous and everyone was worried. The family was sitting down to dinner one night. His wife said that she would just go upstairs for a moment to check on the sick child.

She came down quickly. She said the child was asleep. "But pray go upstairs, for there is a large black dog lying on his bed. Go drive it out of the house." The father knew what that meant. He rushed upstairs. There was no dog to be seen, for the child was already dead.

Not all of these stories of death warnings go back hundreds of years. There is a story connected with the 1924 death of a popular composer named Lionel Monckton.

One evening a group of Monckton's friends were sitting around their club. Monckton, too, was a member of the club. One of his friends, Donald Calthrop, got the feeling that something had happened to Monckton. The others brushed this notion aside. Then Calthrop suddenly fixed his eyes on a corner of the room. "Look!" he shouted. "There is his dog." Monckton often took his dog with him to the club. No one else in the room saw the dog. They thought Calthrop was joking. A few hours later news reached the club that Monckton had died unexpectedly. He had died about the time the dog was seen.

Ernest Bennett, a writer on ghostly subjects, recounted the case of a priest he called Father C. Father C. was waiting for a new assignment. He was staying in a large house. He was the only one in the house except for the servants.

One morning Father C. awoke early. He went downstairs. There he found an old priest

A traditional frightening ghost

staring at him. He did not know who this
priest was or how he had gotten into the
house. Father C. was just about to speak to
the old priest when he vanished.

Father C. asked all the servants who the
old man was. No one else had seen him.
They all insisted that there was no way a

stranger could have gotten into the house.

Five or six weeks later Father C. was assigned to take the place of Father F., who had died recently. When he arrived at his new parish, Father C. saw a large, framed photograph of an elderly priest. Without a doubt it was the same mysterious man he had seen. He asked whose picture it was. The reply was, "Why, don't you know? That was dear Father F."

This ghostly figure did not bring bad luck. Another clergyman did not have such a happy experience. Back in 1777 a certain Rev. James Crawford was crossing a river on horseback. Riding behind him was his sister-in-law, Miss Hannah Wilson. The water was very high. Miss Wilson became frightened and begged Rev. Crawford to turn back.

"I do not think there can be any danger," said Rev. Crawford. "I see another horseman crossing just twenty yards in front of us." Miss Wilson also saw the horseman. Rev. Crawford called out to the other rider.

The rider stopped and turned around. His

face was that of a man no longer human. It was ghostly white and fairly glowed with hate and evil. Rev. Crawford was terrified at the sight and Miss Wilson began to scream. Rev. Crawford turned his horse and got out of the river and back home as quickly as he could.

He was told that this spirit of a rider appeared every time someone was to be drowned in the river. Rev. Crawford had been badly scared. But he felt he should not give in to such superstitions. So he tried to cross the river again. On September 27, 1777, he was drowned in the attempt.

8
THE HANDPRINT
ON THE WALL

Brittish ghost lore is filled with accounts of bloodstains that cannot be washed away. Such a stain is supposed to be the mark of an awful and unavenged crime. America has its own version of this story. It is one of the most popular of all American ghostly tales.

The setting is the coalfields of Pennsylvania during the late nineteenth century. The miners worked under awful conditions. The pay was very low, barely enough to keep a family alive. A man's pay could be cut, or he could be fired without warning. The work itself was

Miners' huts in Pennsylvania in the nineteenth century

backbreaking and dirty. It was also extremely dangerous. Every time a man went into the mines he risked possible death. The mine owners did almost nothing to ensure the safety of their workers. Even those who were not killed outright in mine accidents faced long-term illnesses from coal dust. All food and clothing was purchased at stores owned by the mining companies. Many miners found themselves deeply in debt to the company store.

Most of the miners were poor immigrants.

Inside a Pennsylvania coal mine in the 1850s

They could find no other work. Many recent immigrants from Ireland had come to Pennsylvania to work in the mines. Starting in the 1830s there were rumors that some miners belonged to a secret society called the Molly Maguires. The origin of the name is unknown. There had been such a secret society in Ireland. Its purpose was to protect poor farmers from their landlords.

No one knew much about the Mollies. Even today we don't know too much about them. There were, however, the most frightening rumors. They said that the Mollies were dedicated to sabotage and murder. It was said that the Mollies swore a terrible oath of secrecy. They pledged to kill anyone who opposed them. Those who broke the oath were to be killed immediately.

Supporters of the Mollies said that they were trying to protect the miners. If their names were known they would be fired, and perhaps killed themselves. Opponents charged that the Mollies were just lawless men. They said that the violence was used to settle personal grudges, not to better the conditions of the Irish miners. That controversy goes on today. The Mollies have been called both heroes and villains.

The mine owners hated them. The newspapers printed sensational stories about the Mollies' deeds of violence. Every murder, every explosion, was attributed to them. In the coal-fields there was great fear. No one knew who was a member of the Mollies, and who was a company spy. You could not trust anyone.

In 1873 the mine owners managed to place a spy among the leadership of the Molly Ma-guires. The spy worked secretly for three years. Then he reported what he had found to the mine owners. As a result, many men were arrested and tried. Some nineteen were hanged for murder. Many others were impris-oned.

Was justice done? There is still a dispute. Some contend that many of the men were convicted on trumped-up charges. The mine owners, they say, were not interested in pun-ishing murderers. They wanted to get rid of potential troublemakers among their workers.

It is from this violent period of history that the story of the handprint in cell 17 comes. One of the men arrested as a leader of the Mollies was Alexander Campbell. He owned a small liquor store. Campbell was accused of hiring two men to kill a mine boss.

A meeting of the Molly Maguires

Campbell was tried, along with nine other men. They were all convicted and sentenced to hang. The other men stood silently. Campbell, however, protested his innocence. He continued to insist he was innocent right up to the day of his scheduled execution.

The ten men were to be hung on June 21, 1877. On the fatal morning Campbell rose early. When they came to take him off to the gallows he shouted, "I swear I am innocent!

I was nowhere near the scene of the murder. I had nothing to do with it."

He then struck his hand hard against his cell wall. It left a dark handprint. Campbell shouted, "There is proof of my words! That mark of mine will never be wiped out. There it will remain forever to shame the county that is hanging an innocent man."

It was said in the region that when the ten men were hanged, the sun was suddenly blotted out. Lights all over the county had to be lit. The day of the hangings is called "Black Thursday."

By 1880 many of the leaders of the Mollies had either been executed or were in prison. The organization just faded away. But Alexander Campbell's handprint did not. It stayed there, as fresh as the day it was made on the wall of cell 17.

Many attempts have been made to remove the handprint. One of the wardens of the jail recounted his efforts to wipe out the mark. He used strong soaps, solvents, even a large eraser. Nothing worked. He had doubted the

Leaders of the Mollies hung in Pennsylvania

story until the day he tried to wash away the print. Afterwards, he said he was "quite shaken." He called the whole thing "a mystery."

So Campbell's prophecy about the handprint remaining came true. But what of the second half of the prophecy? Was the county shamed by hanging an innocent man? That is less sure. The handprint has become a tourist attraction. Thousands of people come to the Carbon County jail every year to see it. If the county is ashamed, it is not too ashamed to turn away tourist dollars.

9

THE MURDERER'S SKULL

There have been many tales of murder victims haunting the spot where they were killed. They are looking for vengeance. But here is a tale with a twist. The ghost is that of the murderer. And he is not looking for vengeance. He is looking for his head.

The murder took place in England in 1826. William Corder was seeing a young woman named Maria Marten. Maria was pressing William to marry her. So was her family.

William had other ideas. He had come into a bit of money. Now he wanted to be free of his old girlfriend. He told her they would run off together. They got no farther than a place called the Red Barn. There William shot Maria and buried her under the dirt floor.

William Corder was a stupid man. He really put the noose around his own neck. At first, no one questioned Maria's disappearance. But Corder could not stop talking about her. He even wrote letters about her. Maria's family became suspicious.

Ann Marten, one of Maria's relatives, said she had a dream about Maria. According to Ann, she dreamed that William shot Maria and buried her beneath the floor of the Red Barn. Ann told everybody about her dream. Finally, there was an investigation. The floor of the Red Barn was dug up and Maria's remains were found. The case against William Corder was overwhelming.

It has been suggested that Ann Marten never really had a dream. She suspected what had happened all along. Since she didn't have any evidence, she said she dreamed it all. Others say that Ann Marten really knew what had happened, that she had helped Corder plan the crime. Then she changed her mind and turned him in.

Whatever Ann Marten's reasons, William Corder was brought to trial and found guilty. He was publicly hanged outside the gates of Bury St. Edmunds jail on August 11, 1828.

The people of the early nineteenth century were even more interested in murder than people are today. This case became very famous. Little models of the Red Barn were sold all over England. People flocked to see the real barn.

There is a story about some visitors to the Red Barn. One man came early, when the Red Barn was empty. He went inside. Then he climbed into the grave from which Maria's remains had been taken. Just then two other visitors arrived. They came into the barn. The man in the grave heard them and quickly jumped out. The terrified visitors ran away thinking they had seen poor Maria's ghost.

In 1828 hangings were carried out in public. Everyone for miles around turned out to see the spectacle. After Corder was dead, the hangman sold pieces of the rope to wealthier members of the crowd.

There was worse to come. The bodies of executed criminals were usually sent to medical schools for dissection. Before the medical students got to work, there was a public dissection. Over 5,000 people paid to see the murderer's cut-up remains.

The following day the remains were sent to the West Suffolk General Hospital. There they were completely dissected by medical students. Even at the hospital strange and grisly things were done. A complete account of the trial was made into a book. This book was bound in pieces of Corder's tanned skin. The book still exists today. So does Corder's scalp, which was preserved.

The people of the early nineteenth century were not delicate about death.

Corder's skeleton was used for teaching anatomy. It may still be in use today. But some years after the hanging a Dr. Kilner stole the murderer's skull. He had a spare skull from the anatomy lab put in its place.

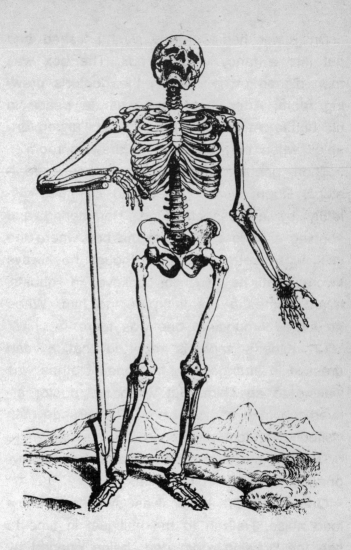

The skeletons of executed criminals were often used for teaching anatomy.

Dr. Kilner had Corder's skull polished and put into a fancy wooden box. The box was then placed on a shelf in the doctor's drawing room. After that there was no peace in his house. At first, people just felt "uncomfortable" when they entered the drawing room.

Then people began hearing strange footsteps. Doors were opened and slammed violently by an unseen hand. Hammering and sobbing sounds came from the box where the skull was kept. The doctor, though he always swore that he did not believe in ghosts, heard someone breathing behind him. When he turned around no one was there.

Dr. Kilner's servants reported that a man dressed in strangely old-fashioned clothes was waiting to see him. But when the doctor arrived the man had vanished. The strange man visited the doctor's house on several more occasions, but always disappeared before anyone got a good look at him.

One night Dr. Kilner was awakened by a loud noise. He ran to the hall just in time to see the drawing room door being opened by a white hand. Just a hand, nothing more.

Suddenly the door was nearly blown off its hinges by an explosion. The doctor rushed into the drawing room, and was met by a gust of icy wind. His candle went out. When he lit a match he saw the skull on the floor grinning at him. The wooden box lay in fragments around it. The skull itself was undamaged. And that was just about enough for Dr. Kilner.

He could not return the skull to the hospital from which he had stolen it. It was so highly polished that it would stand out from the rest of the murderer's skeleton. The theft of the skull would then be known to everyone. So the doctor gave his grim trophy to a Mr. F. C. Hopkins. Hopkins was a retired official of the prison commission. He had bought the old Bury St. Edmunds jail where Corder had been hanged.

Dr. Kilner handed the skull to Hopkins with these words: "Take it as a present. As you own Corder's condemned cell, and the gallows where they hanged him, perhaps it won't harm you to look after his skull."

So the retired prison official wrapped the

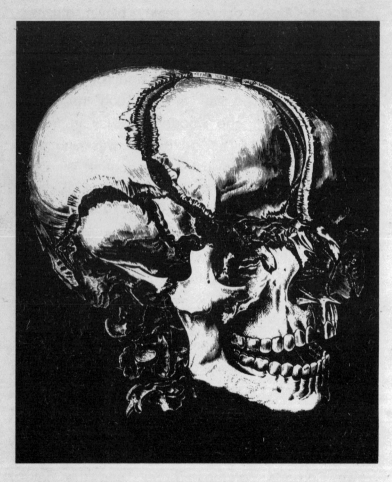

skull in a silk handkerchief and started home.
On the way he fell and sprained his ankle.
The skull rolled out of the handkerchief onto

the ground. A lady who was passing by saw it and promptly fainted.

After that he had nothing but bad luck. Within a few months both Hopkins and Dr. Kilner were bankrupt. They both blamed the evil influence of the skull.

Hopkins decided to break the evil spell. He took the skull to an isolated churchyard. He bribed a gravedigger to give it a proper burial. From that point on the spell of bad luck lifted for both men. The murderer's skull was apparently satisfied.

10

THE GENTLEMAN
FROM AMERICA

Not only are ghosts supposed to be deadly, fear of them can be nearly as deadly. That is the point of this little story, which has been told in many different versions. The time is 1927.

David Bowman was an American visiting England for the first time. Basically David was a good-natured fellow. But he could be rather loud and boastful, particularly when it came to America and Americans. To hear David tell it, everything and everybody in America was better than everything and everybody anywhere else.

David's talk finally began to irritate two of his English friends, Colin MacKenzie and Roger Frost. David was going on at great length about how brave Americans were. "We certainly won the war for you," he told the Englishmen.

"I suppose Americans aren't afraid of ghosts," said Colin.

"Americans don't even believe in ghosts."

"And you wouldn't be afraid to spend the night in a haunted room," continued Colin.

"I told you I don't believe in ghosts."

"Then perhaps we had better tell him about the Drumkettle ghost."

And so they did. Colin's family owned a country estate called Drumkettle. It was said that years ago, long before the estate was the property of the MacKenzie family, a murder had taken place there. A young woman killed her lover when she found him with another woman. She slashed his throat with a knife.

She was hanged for her crime. To the end she expressed no remorse for what she had done. On the contrary, she went to her death saying she would do it again. And, so the story goes, she did. Her spirit returned to Drumkettle. Whenever a man slept in the upstairs bedroom where the murder had taken place, he too was killed by the vengeful ghost. Three men died in that room trying to prove they were not afraid of ghosts.

"No man has slept in that room since my family has owned Drumkettle," said Colin. "If you like, you can be the first."

It was settled. The following weekend David went down to Drumkettle. The house was quite large. The only people who lived there were Colin's younger sister, and his aged mother, who was very hard of hearing. David was warned to say nothing of their plans to mother or sister. His mother would forbid the risky venture if she found out.

After dinner the women retired early, and the three men went upstairs to inspect the haunted room. For a room that was used so rarely it was in good order. It smelled a bit musty, but that did not bother David. The bed

The ghost killed three men who slept in the room.

was clean and comfortable, the room warm, and for a place that was supposed to be haunted, surprisingly cheerful.

Colin pointed to a rope near the bed. "It's an old bellpull," he said. "It still works. If you get in trouble, just pull the rope. It rings a bell downstairs, and Roger and I will come right up."

"I won't need the bell," said David with confidence. And then he added, "If you fellows are thinking of pulling any tricks to scare me, watch out. I brought my own protection." David produced a large and loaded revolver from his pocket.

"I know how to use it," he said. "And I will."

Feeling confident, David readied himself for bed. He settled down to read—a book of ghost stories that he brought himself. That may not have been such a good idea. David really did have strong nerves, and he really didn't believe in ghosts. But being alone in a room that was supposed to be haunted—well, that was bound to make one feel a little uneasy.

As midnight approached David thought he heard sounds. They were footsteps, first faint but growing louder and louder. Then he could hear breathing, coming from just outside the door. Though he still didn't believe in ghosts, he was beginning to feel just a bit frightened, and just a bit insecure in his belief. A woman's voice called softly, "David, David, I am coming for you."

The doorknob turned slowly. David grabbed his gun and rose from the bed to meet whatever it was that was coming. The door did not open. Then directly behind him there was a horrible shriek. David whirled to see a white-draped figure brandishing a bloody knife and screaming, "David, David, I have come for you."

Though terrified, David took careful aim and fired three times. The figure did not fall. It continued to shriek ever more horribly and advance upon him. David crumpled to the floor in a dead faint.

The following morning David was very silent at breakfast. The two Englishmen congratulated him on having survived the evening, and not having pulled the bell cord. David said nothing, but left quickly. And they didn't see or hear from him again for five years.

Then one day, quite without warning, Colin MacKenzie got a letter from David Bowman in America. He said that he was returning to England for the first time in five years, and very much wanted to meet Colin and Roger once again. Colin and Roger were delighted, for they had often talked of David and wondered what had happened to him. Colin wired David to meet them at their club in London, on a particular day.

The day arrived, and so did David, right on time. Five years had aged the three men, but David most of all. When Colin and Roger had last seen David he was a robust young man. Now he looked old. They barely recognized him.

After exchanging a few pleasantries, Roger said something that had been on his mind a long time. "You know we really want to apologize for that trick we played on you. But we were all so young then."

"Trick?" said David.

"Yes, you remember the business with the haunted room. It was all a trick. Colin did the footsteps and the breathing. His sister was in on it. She was the voice. And I was the ghost."

"But how did you get into the room?"

"Drumkettle is an old house," said Roger. "Like a lot of these old places, it has some secret passages. There was a secret passage to the bedroom. It opened behind the wardrobe. I sneaked in while you were looking at the door."

"I shot the ghost three times. How did you manage that?"

"Simple. Blanks. We exchanged your bullets for blanks during the evening. We knew you would have a gun. I wasn't going to risk getting killed."

David sighed and settled back for a moment. Then without warning he sprang forward. A knife was in his hand. He severed Roger's throat with a single slash, and he would have killed Colin as well, if the other men in the room had not grabbed him. It was no easy task. He seemed as strong as ten men, and was raving like a maniac.

Later that night a shattered Colin MacKenzie returned to his rooms. He found another letter from America waiting for him. It was from David's father. The letter warned Colin that David was coming to visit. "He has been ill," said the letter, "very ill for many years. He is only recently out of the institution. I did not want him to go to England, but he insisted and I could not stop him. I know he has often expressed the desire to see you and Roger Frost once again."

"I beg you"—and *beg* was underlined—"not to mention the matter of the ghost. It is the one subject that my poor sick boy cannot abide."

Colin slowly let the letter fall from his hands.

11

THE DREADFUL
SECRET

Many houses have laid claim to the title "the most haunted house in Britain." Glamis Castle has as good a claim to that title as any. But it is a rather strange haunting.

The castle was first built in the fourteenth century. Over the centuries many parts have been added. Older sections were often changed and rebuilt. No one knows what is original and what is reconstruction. Inside the castle is a confusing jumble of rooms and corridors.

The castle has had an evil reputation for a

long time. It is near the spot where King Duncan of Scotland was murdered. His murderer was Macbeth. Shakespeare later made Macbeth famous in a play. But the murder took place before Glamis Castle was built.

In the middle of the fifteenth century the castle was owned by the Second Lord of Glamis. He was known as "the Wicked Lord." He was also called "Earl Beard" because of his long hair and thick whiskers. He spent most of his time drinking and gambling.

There were many stories told about the Wicked Lord. It was said that one Sunday he became very drunk. He roamed up and down the halls looking for someone to play cards with. But no one would play. It was considered a sin to play cards on Sunday.

The Wicked Lord became so angry that he swore he would play cards "with the Devil himself." A short time later there was a loud knock at the door. A tall man wearing a black cloak and big black hat entered. He

Glamis Castle

asked the Wicked Lord if he still wanted a gambling partner. "Yes," roared the Lord, "whoever you are."

The two men went into a room and slammed the door. Their voices could be heard cursing and swearing. The frightened servants crept as close to the room as they dared. They heard the Lord of Glamis complaining he was losing and had nothing left to gamble with. The stranger made a suggestion they could not hear. Whatever it was, the Wicked Lord agreed.

Overcome with curiosity, the butler put his eye to the keyhole of the door. As soon as he did he was nearly blinded by a flash of light. The enraged Lord of Glamis burst from the room. He screamed at his servants for spying on him. But when he turned back to his game, the stranger was gone. And he had taken with him a signed pact for the Lord's soul.

After the Wicked Lord's death, about five years later, people said he still roamed the corridors looking for someone to play cards

Scene from the play *Macbeth*. The play was set near where Glamis Castle was later built.

with. A number of people have reported seeing a bearded ghost at Glamis Castle.

Another ghostly figure reported at Glamis is a woman in gray. This is said to be the ghost of Janet Douglas, wife of James, the Sixth Lord of Glamis.

James died suddenly, and mysteriously, after eating his morning meal. His wife was accused of poisoning him. But no evidence against her could be found, so the case was dropped.

Six years later Janet Douglas was in more serious trouble. This time she was accused of plotting against the King of Scotland. She was also accused of being a witch. There was no way to defend yourself against that accusation. She was executed at Castle Hill in Edinburgh, Scotland, in 1537.

Most of the Lords of Glamis were pretty wild fellows. They drank and gambled away whatever fortunes they had. By 1660 there was almost nothing left. The castle was nearly in ruins. Then the estate was inherited by a very different sort of man. His name was Patrick Lyon. By hard work and thrift he rebuilt the family fortune, and the castle. The King made him Earl of Strathmore. But after Patrick's death his family's old ways reasserted themselves. The later Earls of Strathmore were known as gamblers and drunkards.

By the eighteenth century a new rumor began to circulate about Glamis Castle. It was said that somewhere in the middle of that jumble of rooms and halls was a hidden room. The room was always kept locked. It contained a terrible secret. Only the Earl of Strathmore himself, his heir, and the steward of the castle knew the secret. The secret was revealed to the heir on the evening of his twenty-first birthday.

Usually heirs to the earldom made light of the secret. Then after they became twenty-one they changed. They became very serious and gloomy. One was described by his friends as "a changed man, silent, and moody, with an anxious scared look on his face."

Finally, in 1876 one heir refused to be told

the secret. He did not want to be as frightened by it as his father had been. His wife, however, was curious. She asked the castle steward. He told her gravely, "If your Ladyship did know it, I assure you, you would not be a happy woman."

An 1880 newspaper carried a story about a workman at Glamis. He accidentally knocked a hole in a wall. Behind it was a secret passage. He followed the passage until he came to a hidden locked door. Then the workman became frightened. He told the steward what he had found. A short time later the workman was given a large sum of money. He was told that he should emigrate to Australia. He did, and was never heard from again.

Visitors to the castle have often reported hearing strange noises coming from inside the walls. Even guide books to the castle speak of the "secret."

What is the secret? No one knows. At least those who know are not saying. But there are all sorts of theories.

A haunted castle

According to one theory the room contains the ghost of the Wicked Lord and the Devil, eternally playing cards. Anyone who looks at the scene will be instantly blinded.

Another says it contains Janet Douglas herself. She really was a witch, according to this theory. She has been condemned to live on until the end of the world. Though she is still alive, she is now hideously ancient.

Still another theory says the room contains the skeletons of sixteen people. They were enemies of one of the early Lords of Glamis. He had them walled up in the room where they starved to death.

The most popular theory today holds that the room contained one of the heirs to the estate. According to this theory, the mystery is not hundreds of years old either. It began in 1821. The first-born son of the Eleventh Earl of Strathmore was born severely deformed. He was not expected to live. The family put out the information that the baby died shortly after birth. In reality, the baby was being kept in the secret room.

In time, another son was born. But the deformed older brother was still alive, still in the secret room. He was the rightful heir to the estate. This secret had to be told to all those who wrongfully inherited the earldom. The occupant of the secret chamber lived on for over fifty years. He outlived four Earls of Strathmore. All had to be told of the hidden chamber and what was in it.

People began to mix up this real secret with all sorts of old ghost tales. The Earls of

Strathmore encouraged such confusion. If people were looking for the Wicked Lord and the Devil or an immortal Janet Douglas, they would not guess at the truth.

Is it the truth? No one really knows. People still report hearing strange noises and seeing strange sights at Glamis Castle.

12
WHY DID HE COME BACK?

When you got right down to it, no one really liked Father McSweeney. But no one could explain why.

He was a conscientious and hard-working priest. He attended to the needs of his parishioners. Penniless strangers could always find a meal and a bed at the parish house.

His sermons were correct and well thought out. Perhaps they were a bit chilly. They did not touch the heart. But they showed that much hard work had gone into them.

Long after most of the citizens of the small town in western Ireland had gone to bed, a light could be seen burning in Father McSweeney's window. He seemed to be at work constantly.

What is more, he was not an outsider. He was the son of a farming family that had lived in the area for as long as anyone could remember. Yet even as a boy he had been rather strange and distant. No one much liked him then. Except his mother, of course, and she adored him. When he announced that he wished to go into the priesthood his mother was overjoyed. The people of the neighborhood thought they had seen the last of him. They were wrong. Ultimately he was appointed priest in the parish in which he was born.

People came to him dutifully. But they were never comfortable. Some even felt afraid of him, though they would not admit it. The worst of it was that no one knew why. No one could point to anything that he ever did or said that was wrong. It was just a feeling he gave people.

While he was still a fairly young man, Father McSweeney suddenly took sick. His illness was a mystery. Doctors were called in. They all offered a different opinion. None of them could find a treatment that helped. Through it all Father McSweeney was silent. He acted as if he knew he was going to die. And die he did, within a few weeks of becoming ill. He just wasted away.

Only his aged mother was truly heartbroken. All the others hoped that next time they would be sent a friendlier priest, one who would not make them feel so strange and uncomfortable. In the meantime, Father McSweeney's burial had to be attended to.

Though Father McSweeney was not loved, it was decided to have a big funeral for him. He had, after all, been the priest for years. He also had many relatives in the area. And maybe people felt a bit guilty for not having liked him, though he had served them to the best of his ability.

Father McSweeney's funeral procession started from his mother's house. She was too old and frail to attend the graveside services.

114

But practically everyone else in the area did.
The long procession of cars and carts wound
through the hills up to the cemetery where
Father McSweeney's ancestors had been buried for generations.

The services were long and very formal.
When it was over, people felt more relieved
than sad. All that was left was to travel back
to the priest's mother's house for some food
and drink.

The hour was quite late when the funeral
party left the cemetery. As they started down
the winding road, the sun was setting and the
sky was growing dark.

The returning funeral procession came down
out of the hills into a valley. It was then that
the two men in the lead car saw a lone figure coming along the road toward them. This
was usually a deserted area. Walkers were

rare, especially in the evening.

"Who could that be?" said one of the men.

"We'll see in a moment. He will be in our headlights," replied the driver. The figure drew closer until they could recognize it.

"Lord have mercy on us!" gasped the driver. "It's *himself!*"

The figure on the road was indeed a familiar one. It was someone they had seen for years. It was the figure of the man they had just buried, Father McSweeney. There was no doubt about it. Yet he was changed, horribly changed.

His always pale skin was an ashen white. His eyes were wide open and unblinking. They glittered with an unnatural brightness. His lips were drawn back, exposing strong white teeth and bloodless gums.

This terrifying figure walked the full length of the funeral procession. It did not turn its head or give any other sign of recognition. Everyone, except the few who were dozing, saw it. No one stopped. At first no one said a word. Then the whispers began.

"Did you see him?"

"Yes, I saw him too. I thought I was dreaming."

"So did I. Not dreaming, having a nightmare."

"It couldn't have been him. We buried him. He's dead."

"Well, who, or what, was it, then?"

No one in the procession thought it wise to turn back and follow the ghastly figure. It disappeared down the road. The trembling mourners finally reached the house of Mrs. McSweeney. They all agreed to say nothing. The poor woman had enough grief. She did not need this horrible story.

They knocked at the farmhouse door. There was no reply. They knocked again. Still nothing. Something was wrong. One of the women looked through the window. She saw Mrs. McSweeney lying face down on the floor.

"We'll have to break in," she shouted. And they did. The old woman was not dead. She was unconscious. It took nearly half an hour to bring her around.

"What happened?" they asked.

"I had a visitor," she said. The members of the funeral party shuddered. They now knew where the terrible figure on the road had been coming from.

"A visitor?"

"Yes, there was a knock at the door. I thought everyone was at the funeral. I couldn't think who it might be. So I looked out through the side window, and I saw him— my son. I knew it couldn't be him, but it was."

"You saw his face?"

The old woman hesitated. Then she began to cry. "Yes, I saw his face. It was my son. But he was changed. His face looked so different—so fierce. His features were all twisted. His eyes were wide open and his lips drawn back. And his skin—he was as white as a . . ."

"As a ghost," someone said.

"Yes, I believe I saw the ghost of my son."

"What did you do?"

"I was going to let him in. Ghost or not, he is my son. But as I went to the door my

She saw her dead son looking through the window.

legs became weak. I was so frightened. I must have fainted. But I did see him."

"We believe you," said someone in the group. "We saw him too, on the road just a few miles from here. He must have been walking away from the house."

Father McSweeney was never seen again. But for years people talked about that night. The ghost wore an expression of inhuman cruelty on its face. Perhaps this was something that was hidden in the man's lifetime, yet it lay there just beneath the surface. That may have been why people did not like him, even feared him, though he had done nothing. They sensed the hidden cruelty.

Father McSweeney had always been a secret man. His death and brief reappearance left a fearful mystery.

13

"I'M GOING HOME"

And finally, let me leave you with a tale that is a little less grim.

Today, funerals are pretty cut-and-dried affairs. But at one time, not so very long ago, people got a lot closer to the dead than they usually do now. In some parts of the country it was the custom for relatives, friends, and neighbors to spend the whole night before the burial sitting up with the corpse. The custom has largely disappeared today, but stories from those times are still told now and then.

One of the most popular was about old Zeke. Old Zeke had been crippled and very bent over for most of his life. When he died he was still bent over. He wouldn't fit into his coffin properly. The only way to get him in was to strap him down head and foot.

On the night that folks were sitting up with his corpse, the upper strap suddenly broke. It was just like releasing a spring. The corpse sat straight up in its coffin.

Well, you can imagine what sort of a reaction that produced. Everybody jumped up and ran for the door screaming. But after a moment they recovered a bit. One of the neighbors looked over at the corpse and said, "Look, Zeke, if you're getting up, I'm going home."

INDEX

123

About the Author

DANIEL COHEN is the author of over a hundred books for both young readers and adults, and he is a former managing editor of *Science Digest* magazine. His titles include *Supermonsters*, *The Greatest Monsters in the World*, *Real Ghosts*, *Science Fiction's Greatest Monsters*, and *The Monsters of Star Trek*, all of which are available in Archway Paperback editions. *Ghostly Terrors*, *The World's Most Famous Ghosts*, and *Zoo Superstars* are available from Minstrel Books.

Mr. Cohen was born in Chicago and has a degree in journalism from the University of Illinois. He appears frequently on radio and television and has lectured at colleges and universities throughout the country.